W9-CCL-433
R01617 62315

48 cir
9/08

DUE DATE

THE CHICAGO PUBLIC LIBRARY

AUSTIN-IRVING BRANCH
6100 WEST IRVING PARK
CHICAGO, IL 60634

A VOYAGE TO THE BUNNY PLANET

THE ISLAND LIGHT

Rosemary Wells

DIAL BOOKS FOR YOUNG READERS
NEW YORK

Published by Dial Books for Young Readers
A Division of Penguin Books USA Inc.
375 Hudson Street · New York, New York 10014

Copyright © 1992 by Rosemary Wells
All rights reserved
Printed in the U.S.A.
Design by Atha Tehon
First Edition
1 3 5 7 9 10 8 6 4 2

Library of Congress Cataloging in Publication Data
Wells, Rosemary.
The island light / Rosemary Wells.—1st ed.
p. cm.— (Voyage to the Bunny Planet)
Summary: Felix has an awful day until he is whisked off to the Bunny Planet
to experience the day that should have been.
ISBN 0-8037-1178-6 (lib. bdg.)
[1. Rabbits—Fiction. 2. Sick—Fiction.] I. Title.
II. Series: Wells, Rosemary. Voyage to the Bunny Planet.
PZ7.W46843Is 1992 [E]—dc20 91-41598 CIP AC

THE BUNNY PLANET IN HISTORY

I designated this heavenly body "Coniglio,"
but alas, never saw it again.
Galileo (Diary entry, January 1, 1599)

CHICAGO PUBLIC LIBRARY
AUSTIN-IRVING BRANCH
6100 W. IRVING PK. RD. 60634

Felix was sick in front of the whole art class.

The nurse made him a cup of tea and called home.
Nobody answered the phone.
Felix burned his tongue on the tea.

That afternoon the doctor gave Felix medicine that tasted like gasoline.
Felix's mother and the nurse had to hold him down for a shot.

Later Felix was accidentally soaked by an icy shower.

Felix's father was busy in the cellar with the boiler.
Felix's mother was busy finding a plumber.
Both forgot to kiss him good night.

Felix needs a visit to the Bunny Planet.

Far beyond the moon and stars,
Twenty light-years south of Mars,

Spins the gentle Bunny Planet
And the Bunny Queen is Janet.

"Felix," Janet says. "Come in.

Here's the day that should have been."

The mailboat comes at six o'clock.
I walk my father to the dock.

The boat brings apples, milk, and flour,
And sails back home within the hour.

A squall is stirring up the sky.
Our lighthouse home is warm and dry.

The light was built in nineteen-ten.
It's had six keepers here since then.

We're wet and salty, but who cares?
Our sweaters dry on kitchen chairs.

We mix an apple pancake batter,
Singing while the shutters clatter.

The night wind howls. The rain leaks in.
After supper we play gin.

Our sweaters steam. The fire crackles.
The ocean swells and lifts its hackles.

We split a piece of gingerbread
And play another round in bed.

Outside the sea enfolds the sand.
Inside I hold my father's hand.

Felix wakes at midnight.
Out his bedroom window he sees the Bunny Planet
near the Milky Way in the summer sky.
"It was there all along!" says Felix.

The other two Voyages to the Bunny Planet are:

FIRST TOMATO

MOSS PILLOWS

THE CHICAGO PUBLIC LIBRARY